A Night of Tamales & Roses

Joanna H. Kraus

Pictures by Elena Caravela

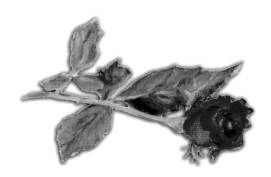

For Tiffany
With special thanks to the East Bay writers for their wise words and support and
to Pete Watson, whose skilled editing made the final version shine.   J. H. K.

For my family with love: Mom, Dad, Avós e Nonni
And for all families, especially those who had a hand in the creation of this book.
E.C.

Text copyright © 2007 by Joanna H. Kraus
Illustrations copyright © 2007 by Elena Caravela

The artwork is rendered in oil on canvas.

Library of Congress Cataloging-in-Publication Data

Kraus, Joanna Halpert.
  A night of tamales and roses / by Joanna H. Kraus ; [illustrations by Elena Caravela].
     p. cm.
  Summary: Ana Luisa is convinced that she has ruined her sister's wedding day when she fails to do her job as
flower girl.
  ISBN 0-9726614-4-1 (hardcover : alk. paper)
  [1. Weddings--Fiction. 2. Sisters--Fiction. 3. Hispanic Americans--Fiction.] I. Caravela, Elena, ill. II. Title.

PZ7.K8675Ni 2007
[E]--dc22

                                    2007016823

Printed in China

For ten days the sewing machine never stopped. From early morning until the sun slid behind the persimmon tree, Ana Luisa's grandmother pinned, cut, basted and stitched.

Her eyes twinkled as she proudly produced a long cloth garment bag. "For the flower girl," she said in Spanish.

Ana Luisa reached to open it.

"Wait," her sister Silvia said, laughing. "Close your eyes."

"And raise your arms," Grandmother added.

Ana Luisa heard the rustle of tissue paper and then felt something soft slip over her T-shirt and shorts. When she looked in the mirror she caught her breath. On the shoulder straps and hem of the sky blue dress, Grandmother had embroidered tiny flowers.

"Gracias, gracias, Abuelita," Ana Luisa said, flinging her arms around her grandmother's waist to thank her. Silvia, in her frothy white wedding gown, kissed them both.

Their grandmother smiled, her eyes moist. *"Dos princesas,"* she murmured. Two princesses.

Later, at the wedding rehearsal, Edward swung Ana Luisa high in the air. "How's my favorite flower girl?" he whispered.

She beamed, glad that tomorrow he'd be her brother. "I've got new white shoes," she told him. "With straps. But I can't wear them 'til Silvia marries you."

Ana Luisa concentrated on walking down the aisle the way she'd been taught. "One. Two," she counted out loud. "Stop, scatter flowers," she whispered to herself.

She held her white wicker basket tightly. *What if I throw too many?* she worried. *What if there's none left for the end?*

Afterwards, all the bridesmaids and ushers and *Mamá* and *Papá* hugged her.

"*Perfecto*." *Abuelita* said.

The next morning Ana Luisa helped *Mamá* put raisins in hundreds of tamales. The fragrant aroma made her hungry. She eyed the corn husk squares stuffed with chicken, olives and cinnamon-scented rice. *Mamá* smiled and gave her a taste from one that was broken. "But the rest," she warned, "are for the wedding reception."

By late afternoon aunts, uncles and cousins had arrived. Soon the hall table became a tower of envelopes and silver-bowed packages.

Then it was time to get ready.

Grandmother fastened the hooks and eyes on Ana Luisa's dress. *Mamá* unbraided Ana Luisa's hair, brushing it behind her ears with a large, silver-backed brush. "You look beautiful," she murmured, adding a blue-flowered headband. "But remember, it's your sister's day." She kissed the top of her head. "One day it will be yours."

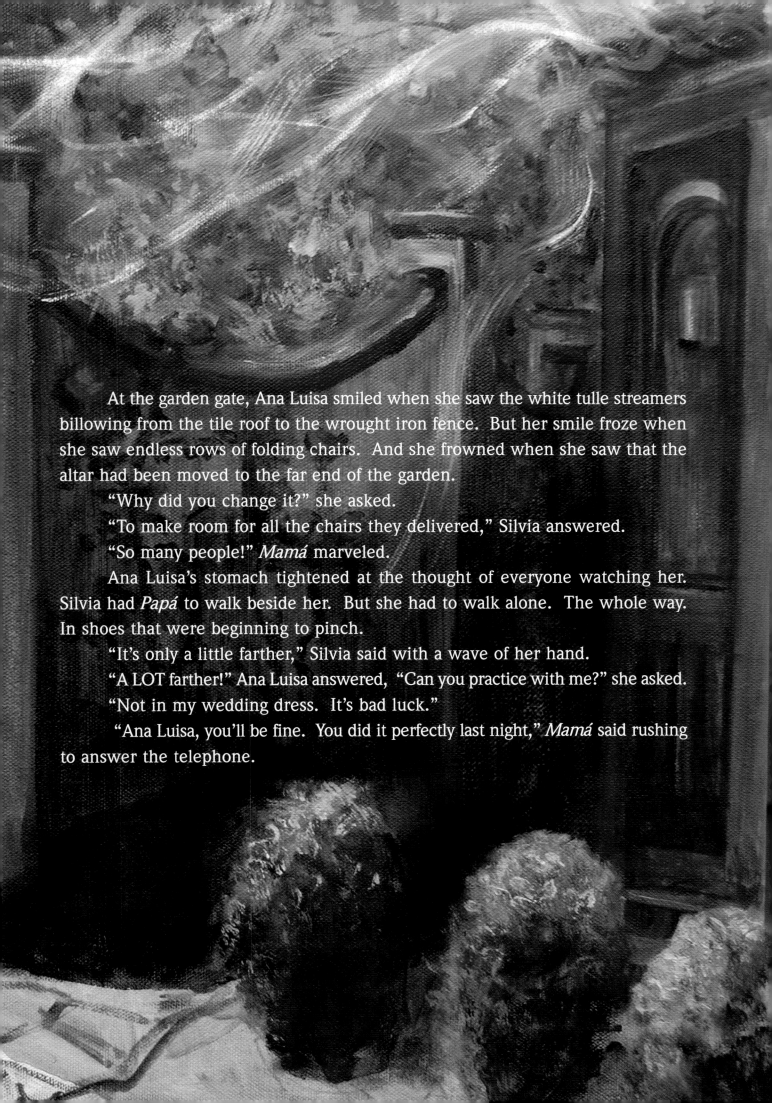

At the garden gate, Ana Luisa smiled when she saw the white tulle streamers billowing from the tile roof to the wrought iron fence. But her smile froze when she saw endless rows of folding chairs. And she frowned when she saw that the altar had been moved to the far end of the garden.

"Why did you change it?" she asked.

"To make room for all the chairs they delivered," Silvia answered.

"So many people!" *Mamá* marveled.

Ana Luisa's stomach tightened at the thought of everyone watching her. Silvia had *Papá* to walk beside her. But she had to walk alone. The whole way. In shoes that were beginning to pinch.

"It's only a little farther," Silvia said with a wave of her hand.

"A LOT farther!" Ana Luisa answered, "Can you practice with me?" she asked.

"Not in my wedding dress. It's bad luck."

"Ana Luisa, you'll be fine. You did it perfectly last night," *Mamá* said rushing to answer the telephone.

But when Ana Luisa ran outside to practice, she was swallowed up by aunts and uncles instead, who hugged her and said how grown up she looked.

She didn't feel grown up.

When Edward grinned, lifting her high above his shoulders, she didn't grin back. From that height she could see more and more cars snaking down the street. *Who are all those people?* she wondered. She gulped as the garden gate swung open again. *They're all coming HERE!*

Soon flute and guitar music filled the air. Ushers led guests to their seats.

It was time for the ceremony.

But when Ana Luisa ran to her entrance spot, she tripped on the cement path. Her basket toppled. Rose petals fell out. Tiny red drops trickled down her bare arm. Her eyes filled with tears.

Grandmother flew over. "*¡Oye!*" From her bag she pulled out a clean handkerchief and wiped off the scratch, then dashed back to her seat.

Ana Luisa looked down. There were big, ugly scuffs across the fronts of her shoes. Now everyone would know she tripped. What if she fell again? What if they laughed?

"Ready?" Silvia whispered urgently from behind the screen door.

"I have to go to the bathroom," Ana Luisa stalled.

"Afterwards," Silvia answered, pushing her sister gently. "Listen, there's our music.

"I have to go *now*," Ana Luisa pleaded, running into the small powder room.

In the powder room she took a paper towel and rubbed at the scuffs on her new white shoes. But no matter how she tried, they didn't look brand new again. She wanted to stay in this safe, quiet room forever.

"Hurry up!" Silvia called.

Ana Luisa trembled as she walked back. Bravely, she took the first two steps. As the music grew louder, everyone turned in their seats to see the flower girl. But when she looked at all those strangers, her knees wobbled. Terrified, she stopped.

"Go, Ana Luisa. Please go!" Silvia begged. "For me. For Edward. For *Mamá*. For *Papá*. For *Abuelita!*"

But Ana Luisa's feet wouldn't move. A big tear rolled down her cheek.

　　With a great sigh, Silvia pushed past, took her father's arm and glided down the red-carpeted aisle.

　　She heard "Ooohs" and "Ahhhs" as the beautiful bride floated past. Embarrassed, she scrunched down in back and covered her face. Then, slowly, between her fingers, she peeked out at the ceremony.

　　She was sure Silvia would never speak to her again. Edward would never swing her up in the air. She had ruined their wedding. Miserably, she crouched under a chair. She wondered if she could stay there until all the guests had gone home.

But when Silvia swept by, she paused, looked down and held out her hand for her little sister.

"Come with us," she said kissing her on the cheek.

"You're still my favorite flower girl," Edward winked, taking her other hand.

As they stood in the reception line, *Abuelita* gave her a swift hug.

"*¡Felicitaciones!* Congratulations!" The words flew around her like confetti.

Then she saw *Mamá* bringing out the platters of hot tamales she helped make.

When the dance band began, her feet swung to the sound. Edward scooped her up and twirled her about the lawn. Holding her basket high, she finally scattered her rose petals into the crowd.

Ana Luisa and her family and all the guests ate and danced until the moon came out, the stars shone, and there wasn't one tamale left.